Kylie Jean

Pirate Queen

by Marci Peschke

illustrated by Tuesday Mourning

PICTURE WINDOW BOOKS

a capstone imprint

Kylie Jean is published by Picture Window Books
A Capstone Imprint
1710 Roe Crest Drive
North Mankato, Minnesota 56003
www.capstoneyoungreaders.com

Library of Congress Cataloging-in-Publication Data
Peschke, M. (Marci)
 Pirate queen / by Marci Peschke ; illustrated by Tuesday Mourning.
  p. cm. -- (Kylie Jean)
 Summary: Inspired by her report on a female pirate, and challenged by a boy in her class, Kylie Jean and her friends decide to form a pirate gang, complete with costumes, a secret hideout, and buried treasure--but when the treasure disappears Kylie makes an important discovery about the local haunted house.
 ISBN 978-1-4048-7581-4 (library binding) -- ISBN 978-1-4048-8103-7 (paper over board) -- ISBN 978-1-4795-1529-5 (ebook) -- ISBN 978-1-4795-8020-0 (paperback)
 1. Pirates--Juvenile fiction. 2. Treasure troves--Juvenile fiction. 3. Elementary schools--Juvenile fiction. 4. Friendship--Juvenile fiction. [1. Pirates--Fiction. 2. Buried treasure--Fiction. 3. Elementary schools--Fiction. 4. Schools--Fiction. 5. Friendship--Fiction.] I. Mourning, Tuesday, ill. II. Title. III. Series: Peschke, M. (Marci) Kylie Jean.
 PZ7.P441245Pir 2013
 813.6--dc23   2012028534

Graphic Designer: Kristi Carlson
Editor: Beth Brezenoff
Production Specialist: Eric Manske

Design Element Credit:
Shutterstock/blue67design

Printed in China.
001250

For Sophie, with love for Rick
—MP

Table of Contents

All About Me, Kylie Jean!

My name is Kylie Jean Carter. I live in a big, sunny, yellow house on Peachtree Lane in Jacksonville, Texas with Momma, Daddy, and my two brothers, T.J. and Ugly Brother.

T.J. is my older brother, and Ugly Brother is . . . well . . . he's really a dog. Don't you go telling him he is a dog. Okay? I mean it. He thinks he is a real true person.

He is a black-and-white bulldog. His front looks like his back, all smashed in. His face is all droopy like he's sad, but he's not.

His two front teeth stick out, and his tongue hangs down. (Now you know why his name is Ugly Brother.)

Everyone I love to the moon and back lives in Jacksonville. Nanny, Pa, Granny, Pappy, my aunts, my uncles, and my cousins all live here. I'm extra lucky, because I can see all of them any time I want to!

My momma says I'm pretty. She says I have eyes as blue as the summer sky and a smile as sweet as an angel. (Momma says pretty is as pretty does. That means being nice to the old folks, taking care of little animals, and respecting my momma and daddy.)

But I'm pretty on the outside and on the inside. My hair is long, brown, and curly.

I wear it in a ponytail sometimes, but my absolute most favorite is when Momma pulls it back in a princess style on special days.

I just gave you a little hint about my big dream. Ever since I was a bitty baby I have wanted to be an honest-to-goodness beauty queen. I even know the wave. It's side to side, nice and slow, with a dazzling smile. I practice all the time, because everybody knows beauty queens need to have a perfect wave.

I'm Kylie Jean, and I'm going to be a beauty queen. Just you wait and see!

Chapter One
Talk Like a Pirate

Ahoy, mateys! This is an exciting time for me and my friends. Halloween is coming, and I have been getting ready for my biography book report.

Can you guess who my report is going to be about? I just gave you a little clue.

If you think I'm reporting on a pirate, then you're sure good at guessing! I checked out books from my school library and from the public library to learn everything I can about my lady pirate.

She's an Irish, red-haired pirate queen, Grace O'Malley.

I am up early for a Friday morning. Sometimes it's harder to wake up than it is to find buried treasure, but today I need to make a hat for my book report before I eat breakfast.

Momma shouts, "Kylie Jean, T.J., are you up yet?"

"Aye, I am!" I reply.

I can hear T.J. snoring while I put the final touches on my hat. Momma yells again, louder this time. "T.J. Carter, you better get up or you'll be late for school!"

I put my hat on and look in the mirror. I gasp. "Blimey!" I say. "I look just like a pirate queen."

Ugly Brother barks. "Ruff, ruff." That means he agrees!

"In two more weeks, it will be Halloween," I tell him. "Look at me. I'm gonna be a pirate!"

The pirate hat I made looks pretty amazing. I used black construction paper and made a pink glitter skull and crossbones. On my way out the door, I spy my pink feather boa, so I pluck out a pink feather and stick it in the side of my creation. "Perfect!" I say, taking one more peek in the mirror. Then I head downstairs.

Momma is pouring orange juice when I walk into the kitchen.

"Pirates got a disease called scurvy because they didn't eat oranges while they were sailing on the high seas," I tell her. I grab my glass of juice and drink it all down.

"Really?" Momma asks.

"Aye," I reply.

I pour my cereal into a white bowl with a little gold crown on the front. Granny gave it to me for my birthday.

"Your brother had better get up soon," Momma says. "Guess he's pretty tired from helping out at the Pettigrews' last night."

"Helpin' them with what?" I ask.

"Oh, his youth group has been mowing lawns and helping out around people's houses," Momma says. "And that's great, but he still needs his sleep."

T.J. wanders in with his hair sticking up all over. He yawns and stretches. Then he looks at me. Quick as a wink, he takes a second look.

He groans. "Please tell me you are not gonna wear that silly hat on the bus," he says.

I nod. "Aye!" I tell him. "Wearin' this hat is part of my homework."

Momma asks, "Is talkin' like a pirate part of your homework, too?"

I shrug. "Not really, but it's fun!" I say.

Before anyone else can say anything, we hear Mr. Jim, our bus driver, honk twice.

"Ahoy!" I say. "We better hurry!"

T.J. has to grab some toast because he slept too long to get anything else. Momma tries to squish down his crazy hair, but there's no time! We grab our lunches and run out the door.

When I get to school, I see my best cousin, Lucy. She is wearing a cowgirl hat. Her report is about Annie Oakley, the famous Wild West sharpshooter.

When Lucy sees my pirate hat, we both laugh.

"This is just like what Pa always says," Lucy tells me. "Great minds think alike."

Right after the morning announcements, our teacher starts our book report presentations. I want to go first, but Ms. Corazón follows her class list. Since Carter begins with the letter C, I will be fourth.

My friend Cole goes first, since his last name is Adams. His report is about Jacques Cousteau, an underwater scientist. I can hardly wait for my turn.

Finally, Ms. Corazón calls, "Kylie Jean Carter. Your turn."

I stand at the front of the room in my pirate hat and begin my report.

"Ahoy, mateys!" I say. "My report is about the red-haired pirate queen Grace O'Malley. Grace was born in 1530. She was a lady buccaneer, so they called her the Pirate Queen. Y'all know how much I love queens!"

"She fought off fierce pirates with her cutlass," I go on. "In case ye don't know, a cutlass is a curved sword used by pirates. There were two hundred men under her command! She had twenty pirate ships. They sailed the seas hunting Spanish and English ships to steal treasure from. As part of her booty — that's pirate for treasure — she owned castles and piles of gold doubloons."

"Grace was held in the dungeons of Dublin Castle," I say. "A dungeon is like a jail. Grace even met her enemy, the Queen of England, to make peace and to free her son and brother."

I take a breath, and then go on. "Grace was married and had four children," I say. Women in the old days didn't have much freedom, but she proved that you could do anything if you put your mind to it. She was even the leader of her Irish clan. Some called her the Dark Lady. She died in 1603."

Ms. Corazón says, "Very good, Kylie Jean. That was a fascinating report. You deserve a gold star!"

The girls clap and cheer, especially Lucy, Cara, and Paula. The boys in the class are shocked. Cole blurts out, "Girls can't be pirates!"

Ms. Corazón warns us, "Students, please remember to raise your hand if you want to speak, and I will call on you. Now it's time for Lucy's book report."

When I sit down, Cole sticks his tongue out at me. Can you believe it?

I just have to prove that girls can be pirates. I want to be a pirate queen just like Grace O'Malley!

Chapter Two
Swing from a Rope

Later that afternoon on the playground, Cole and the other boys tease me about my report.

"Kylie Jean is no pirate queen!" Cole shouts. "Girls can't be pirates!"

It makes me so mad! I yell, "If I was a pirate queen, I'd make you walk the plank!"

My girlfriends and I look at each other. "We have to think of a way to prove that girls can be pirates," I say. "And in time for Halloween, because that's my costume!"

"That's right," Cara says.

"But what can we do?" Lucy asks.

We swing and think. It's really hard! We don't have any pirate treasure or a ship. Then Cara's eyes squeeze shut. "I have an idea!" she says. "Let's have a sword fight."

"That's a great idea!" I shout. I have an older brother and a younger dog brother, so I've seen about a hundred pirate movies. I know how they dance around with a sword.

I march over to Cole and say, "I challenge you to a pirate sword fight!"

"What?" he says, looking confused.

"If I win, you have to admit that girls make great pirates. Got it?" I say.

"Um, okay," Cole says. "What can we use for swords?"

I spy some long dried-out sticks on the edge of the playground. They sort of look like swords. "Those sticks will be fine," I say. Paula runs over and grabs a handful.

I figure I'm going to get real dirty. You know beauty queens do not like to get dirty! However, being a farm girl, I also know that sometimes getting dirty is part of the job. And besides, real true pirates don't worry too much about staying clean.

Cara hands us each a sword. I shake some dirt off of mine. "Stand back to back until I shout start," Cara says. "Then walk ten steps, turn around and use your sword. Got it?"

My heart is thumping. "Got it," I growl.

Cole bellows, "Me, too!"

We turn back to back. His back feels like a bag of skeleton bones against mine. Then Cara shouts for us to start.

As we take our paces, we count. At the tenth step, we turn.

I run at him and he runs at me! We are both really brave, but the minute our swords hit each other, they break into itty bitty pieces. Standing there with our broken swords, we are both surprised.

"Now what?" Cole asks.

Lucy thinks fast. "Maybe we should see which pirate can walk the plank," she suggests.

Cole and I are going to walk across the teeter-totter. The pirate who makes it across the plank without quitting or getting scared wins the bet.

My feet are steady. I balance as I move quickly across the plank. The girls all clap and Paula cheers, "Ta-da!"

The problem is that Cole steps right on that plank and walks straight across it, too. Then the boys clap and cheer. Blimey! I want to prove to the boys that I'm as good a pirate as Cole.

Cole's friend Justin says, "Kylie Jean, if you think you can be a pirate, then prove it. Swing from a rope!"

Three long ropes dangle down from the tip-top of the monkey bars. Cole touches all three of the ropes like he's testing them.

He spits into his hands and rubs them together, grabbing on to the middle rope. Beauty queens never spit! Just because I want to be a pirate queen does not mean I'm going to take up spitting.

Cole runs back as far as he can pull the rope, jumps up, and swings through the air. I do the same and swish past him like a real true swashbuckler.

The boys are still not convinced, but before I can challenge them to another pirate battle, the recess bell rings. When we line up, Cole is standing behind me. He whispers, "Kylie Jean, YOU are not a pirate!"

Boys are a bunch of scurvy dogs. There has to be a way I can prove I'm a pirate queen.

And before you know it, I think of a great plan!

Chapter Three
A Pirate Crew and Code

On Saturday afternoon, I invite my best cousin Lucy and my other friends to come to my house.

Aunt Susie brings Lucy early. She and Momma will have a chat while we play. Nanny likes to say that sisters can always find things to talk about. Sometimes I wish Ugly Brother was a girl so I could have a sister, too. Lucy is so lucky to have a sister. But now I have a pirate queen plan. If it works out, I'll have a pirate crew. Pirate crews are even better than sisters!

Lucy and I go upstairs to play while we wait for our other friends. "I thought your report was awesome!" she tells me. "Your costume will be great for Halloween."

"The boys didn't think it was any good," I say. Then I add, "Wait until everyone gets here and I'll tell y'all about my big plan."

We don't have to wait too long before the rest of the girls come knocking on the door. Then we run out into the backyard. We all sit at Momma's picnic table.

I wait till everyone is quiet. Then I ask, "What does every pirate captain need?"

Paula frowns. "Is this a pirate joke?" she asks.

"No way!" I say. "I'm serious."

The girls look at each other. Then Lucy says, "I give up. Tell us what every captain needs."

Cara shouts, "I've got it! A crew, right?"

"Shiver me timbers!" I exclaim. "Ye figured it out!" I look over at my cousin. "Lucy, will you be my first mate?" I ask.

Lucy winks and says, "Aye!"

I continue, "Cara, you can be the old salt."

Cara gets a disgusted look on her face. "The what?" she asks.

"The old salt. The experienced sailor," I explain. "Since you have been sailing on your uncle's sailboat. You have experience."

"Okay," Cara says, but she doesn't look too sure.

"What about me?" Paula asks.

I think for a minute and then say, "I know! You can be the cabin boy."

"I'm not a boy," Paula complains. "What else is left?"

"The cook," I say.

Paula sighs. "I guess I'd rather be the boy than the cook," she says.

"The cabin boy helps out around the ship," I explain. "You don't have to be a boy to do that job." I look around. "That means you're the cook, Ugly Brother," I tell my dog.

He whines and barks once. That means no!

"I'll try to find you a better job," I promise him.

"What do we do to start?" Lucy asks.

"Well, I think the first thing we have to do is make our own pirate code," I say.

I explain that pirates lived by a code. The code is a set of rules that each mate promises to follow. We will all have to take an oath. Together we make our very own pirate code.

"Every mate gets a vote," I say.

"Okay," Cara says, "but only as long we all get to take turns wearing the pirate hat."

That gives me a great idea! "Everyone in the crew should make their own hat," I say. All the girls cheer.

"What other rules can we have in the code?" Paula asks. "How about, no one leaves the crew, ever, even if they move?"

"That's a good one!" I say.

"What did real pirates have on their list?" Lucy asks.

I tell her, "Real pirates had lights out by eight, so that can be on our list, too."

"My bedtime is at eight anyway," Lucy says.

"Mine too," I say. "So it's perfect!"

"We should add that we can stay up late on special occasions," Cara says. "You know. Just in case."

"That's a good idea," I say.

"That seems like enough rules," Cara says.

I nod and say, "Let's all vote. Say aye if you like the rules, and say nay if you don't."

At the same time, we all say, "Aye!"

Lucy, my first mate, writes down our code.

1. All mates get a vote.

2. All mates get a turn.

3. All mates make their own hats.

4. No fighting.

5. No quitting.

6. Lights out by eight
   (except on special occasions).

Each girl sits on a log and swears to follow the code. Real pirates sat on the cannon, but since we don't have one, the log will have to do. Then we all sign our new pirate code with my sparkly gold pen.

"Ahoy, me mateys!" I say. "Now we are a real pirate crew!"

Chapter Four
Every Pirate Needs a Parrot

On Sunday after church, Lucy and I talk like pirates all the way to Nanny and Pa's Lickskillet Farm for Sunday lunch. We are excited about our brand-new pirate crew, but something seems to be missing.

Lucy asks, "Do you think we need a cook?"

"No, not really," I reply. "We can always eat crackers." Then I add, "How about a parrot, matey?"

Lucy agrees, "Aye, me hearty, that is just what we need!"

Before we can say anything else, T.J. starts to complain! "Can't you two talk like normal girls?" he asks.

"Are you telling me to pipe down, bucko?" I reply.

He doesn't answer me. Instead, he says, "Momma! Make her stop doing that."

Momma just laughs. "It's good to know two languages," she says.

T.J. can't help it. He starts to laugh, too. I have to say, I don't think pirate talk is all that funny.

Lucy and I ignore them. We have been thinking hard about our parrot problem.

Then an idea hits me like gold in a treasure chest. I have a brother who loves pirates! Not T.J., Ugly Brother. He will be a parrot for our crew! I tell Lucy, and we decide to sing a sea shanty to celebrate our good fortune in getting a full crew. Our song goes like this:

Oh, I'm a pirate and have one leg!

I have one eye!

A hook for an arm and a yo ho hi!

I sail the seas on my pirate ship.

If I see you and you see me,

You better sail fast!

Then we start all over again. Daddy turns onto Lickskillet Road. We are almost to Nanny and Pa's farm, so we stop singing. I think T.J. is glad.

Momma asks, "Where did you hear that pirate song?"

"I just made it up," I say.

T.J. shakes his head.

* * *

When I get home, I make Ugly Brother a special dog collar with bright paper feathers tied all around it.

Then I carefully tie it around his neck and I take a real good long look at him.

He has the body of a fat ol' bulldog, but at least he has the colors of a parrot.

I explain, "You are one lucky sailor! From now on, you get to be the parrot instead of the cook."

He barks, "Ruff."

One bark means no, so he is not convinced.

"Come on, no one wants to be the cook," I say. "Please? You can eat crackers and help us find a secret pirate hideout. . . ."

He barks, "Ruff, ruff."

Ugly Brother sure loves crackers.

Chapter Five
Treasure Island

The crew and I decide that we need a secret pirate cove, so we all agree to meet after school the next day at my house. As soon as we're all there, I suggest, "Maybe the woods behind Granny and Pappy's house would work. It's very secret."

"How about your garage?" Lucy asks.

Cara groans. "Those are too boring," she says. "Someplace a little mysterious might make a better hideout."

"I know!" Paula says. "How about the spooky old house at the end of Kylie Jean's street?"

I know the house she means. People call it the Black house, because the last person to live there was an old man named Bart Black.

"I love that idea," Cara says. "The boys will never find us if we make our hideout there!"

When I look at Lucy, I can tell she is scared. She thinks the house is haunted.

It is creepy. No one lives there, but sometimes it looks like the old curtains are moving, as if someone is looking out. Some of the windows have boards over them. The white paint on the house is all peeling off, showing the gray wood underneath. Plus, it's Halloween time. Everything is creepier around Halloween!

Lucy shivers. "I'm not going!" she says. "That house is creepy. Everyone says it's haunted!"

"There are no haunted houses in Jacksonville," I say, putting my hands on my hips. "Don't worry, Lucy." I sure hope I'm right!

Cara smiles and adds, "Remember, the Black house is just a house."

"I know it's a house," Lucy says. "An old, dark, spooky house!"

Paula stands up. "Come on," she says. "Let's go before it gets dark and we have to go home."

After packing a few things in our treasure chest, which is really just a cardboard box, I call our parrot and we set out down the street. We look like a little parade.

I am in the front with my parrot, Ugly Brother, ahead of me. Then comes the crew in their pirate hats, and at the end my first mate, Lucy, pulling the treasure chest in a wagon. I think Lucy wants to be last in line. She's as scared as a pirate on a plank.

Before long, we march right up to our new hideout. I look up at the old house and think I see something in the window upstairs. Lucy has got my imagination running wild.

Cara starts to wade through the long, dry grass toward the back of the house.

"Hey, where are you going?" I shout.

She hollers back, "Exploring. It might be hard to get inside the house."

I don't say anything, but I decide it's a pretty good idea, so I follow her. Paula follows me.

"Don't leave me here all alone with Ugly Brother!" Lucy calls nervously.

Ugly Brother whines. But we just keep going anyway.

As Paula, Cara, and I turn the corner, we see an old shed. The windows are so dirty I can't see inside, so I rub my sleeve on the glass until I can see a small, dirty room.

Perfect! The boys will never look for us here. Paula pulls open the rusty door and it creaks and groans.

Behind us, we hear Lucy shriek, "What's that noise?"

"Just the door!" Paula shouts. "Come on, it's safe!"

Now that we've found our secret spot, the crew needs to vote for or against it. If you think Lucy votes nay, you're right. "No way," she says, looking at the shed. "The garage will be much better."

Everyone else votes aye. Ugly Brother votes "ruff, ruff." I count his vote as an aye, too. The vote is four in favor and one against! Lucy's vote is outnumbered, and so our hideout will be behind the old Black house.

Lucy blows out a great big sigh and starts to unpack the treasure chest. Paula and Cara begin to move old, dusty pots and watering cans out of the shed.

I hide everything so that no one even knows we've been there. We leave the dirty windows dark so the boys can't find us!

While we work, I have a funny feeling someone is watching us. It might be a good idea not to tell Lucy or the crew.

We set all of our water bottles on an old shelf next to our tin of crackers. We put our treasure chest box in the middle of the room. Inside, gold bead necklaces and fake gold coins glimmer in the dim light.

In one corner, there is an old rusty metal bucket. Upside down, it makes a great stool, so I sit right on it. Lucy and Paula pull the wagon inside the shed to use as their seat.

Cara finds a little wooden bench that is kind of wobbly. She says, "Every time this bench wobbles, it makes me feel like I'm sailing on an ocean full of waves."

I nod. "Being here makes me feel like we sailed right over to our very own treasure island!" I tell them.

Paula passes around the crackers. Pirates would call them hardtack. Next, we all have a swallow of water.

I teach the other girls the pirate song, and we sing it together until our parrot dog begins to howl. Then we pass our water bottle around again.

Outside, the sun is starting to float like a big orange ball as it goes down to make room for the moon, and inside, we can barely see. As the captain, I have to look out for my crew.

"We have to go back now before it gets dark," I say. Then I give the orders. "Prepare to set sail!" I shout.

Paula asks, "What does that mean in pirate talk?"

"Get your stuff," I tell her.

We pack up quickly. As we are walking around the old house, Lucy stops. She is right behind me and everyone else is behind her. The other girls both have to stop.

Cara asks, "Why are we stopping?"

"A . . . a . . . a . . . light," Lucy stammers, pointing at the house.

I spin around and see a light in one of the windows. Then quick as a flash, it is gone. Now I wonder if I really saw it at all. "It's probably just the sun reflecting on the window," I say, though I'm not really sure. "Come on. Let's go!"

I start walking a little faster. The crew walks faster, too. Even our dog parrot speeds up! Seeing the light was kind of spooky, but a pirate captain can't be a 'fraidy cat. It was just my imagination playing tricks on me. Right?

Chapter Six
The Gold Hoop

I've been reading up on pirates so that I can prove to Cole that girls can be pirates, and also so I can get ready for Halloween. Lots of pirates wore a gold hoop earring. Some pirates even wore two. That makes me want to get my ears pierced.

I learned something else, too! There was a famous pirate named Black Bart.

I wonder if he could be related to Bart Black, who used to own the Black house, where we made our pirate hideout.

I decide to ask Momma if I can go to the mall on Saturday and get my ears pierced. I'm as nervous as a captain without a crew, because I'm pretty sure Momma is going to say no. That means I have to be ready to beg.

The next day at school, I tell Lucy all about my plan. I say, "I'm goin' to get my ears pierced so I can look like a real pirate."

Lucy gasps. "Your momma is gonna let you get pierced ears?" she asks. "No way!"

I fidget with the books on my desk. "She might say yes," I say hopefully.

Lucy shakes her head. My momma is her aunt, so she knows she is strict. Momma always says she doesn't want me to grow up too fast, but my pirate costume won't look very good without earrings!

I just have to talk Momma into letting me get them.

"Can you help me think of some good reasons to get pierced ears?" I ask Lucy.

Lucy frowns and wrinkles her nose. She's thinking hard. "Hmmm," she says. "Maybe there aren't any good reasons."

I can only think of one. "If I do it now, then I won't have to do it later," I say. "Right?"

Lucy smiles. "If you have them pierced, then you'll have to keep them clean," she says, eyes twinkling. "Parents like to give us jobs to do. It makes us more responsible."

"That's a good reason!" I say. "Can you think of any more?"

Lucy shrugs. "Not really," she says. "Ask Cara."

Cara is busy finishing her math homework, so she can't worry about earrings. I have all afternoon to think about it, but I still can't think of anything. I ask Ugly Brother, but he isn't much help. He doesn't do much talking, usually just yes and no.

* * *

I don't get up the nerve to ask Momma about the pierced ears until Friday.

Friday means pizza for dinner. I'm in my room reading when I hear the doorbell, and then I smell some spicy pepperoni. Before Momma calls us, I already know it's time to eat.

When everyone sits down to eat, I can't wait any longer to ask Momma, so I blurt out, "I need pierced ears so I can be a real true pirate for Halloween. Please say yes!"

Momma makes the same face she does when Ugly Brother has an accident in the house. Taking a deep breath, she puts both of her hands on the table. "Kylie Jean Carter, " she begins.

She used all of my names! This is not a good sign. Under the table, Ugly Brother whines. Even he can tell that Momma is not happy.

"You are too young for pierced ears," Momma begins. "Besides, it really hurts when they punch your ears with that piercin' gun, and they're a lot of work to take care of. Sometimes the holes even grow shut."

I start to talk, but Momma holds her hand up. "I think sixteen is the perfect age for gettin' your ears pierced," she says. "I'm sorry, Kylie Jean, but you will have to be a pirate without pierced ears."

"Please, please, please, Momma," I beg. "It will help me learn to be responsible. I know I will have to clean my earrings every day. If I do it now, then I won't have to do it later when I'm sixteen. Lots of girls at school have their ears pierced. Cara does. And you know all the beauty queens do, too!"

Momma sighs. "You are my daughter," she tells me. "Those other girls are not my children. Not everyone has them. Lucy doesn't have pierced ears, and neither does Paula."

I look across the table at Daddy and say, "Pretty please, Daddy?"

He shakes his head no. He will not cross Momma. If Momma says no, then his answer is no, too!

I am so sad I can hardly eat my pizza.

T.J. grins at me. "Don't worry, Lil' Bit," he says. "You'll be sixteen before you know it."

He's trying to make me feel better, but I am soooo disappointed. The rest of the weekend, I'm sadder than a pirate stuck on land.

* * *

On Monday, things get even worse. When I get to school, I find out that Paula's aunt took her to the mall to get her ears pierced on Saturday. Now Paula has a small gold post in each ear. Her baby sister got her ears pierced, too! Can you believe it?

"In six weeks, I can change the posts," Paula says. "I already got a pair to switch to." She shows us the little gold box.

You guessed it. Inside the box are two perfect small gold hoops. Pirate hoops!

I've never felt so sad in my life!

Chapter Seven

Peg Leg

Thank goodness our teacher has a surprise for the class. Pirate hoops will have to wait. Our class has a new pet goldfish! This is such exciting news that I don't have time to think about getting my own ears pierced.

"We're going to have a special contest," says Ms. Corazón. She writes on the board in her fancy writing: Name Our Fish. "Whoever comes up with the best name will win a prize."

"Who decides the best name?" I ask.

Our teacher smiles. "You all will," she says.

For the rest of the morning, we try to think of names for our new fish.

We watch him swish through the water in his big glass fishbowl. It has teeny tiny gold stones in the bottom and a little fake treasure chest.

"Look in the fishbowl!" I say. "There's a little treasure chest. That fish is the perfect pet for a pirate like me!"

"Girls can't be pirates," Cole says.

We all ignore him. Lucy says, "I think we should name him Swimmy. He likes to swim."

"Yeah, but all fish like to swim," Cara says.

Billy likes Sushi and Bait for names. Lucy shakes her head. "Those are mean names," she says.

Then Billy suggests Fin, and Cole shouts, "Yeah!"

Another kid likes Charlie, but nobody thinks that name would be good for a fish.

Then an idea hits me like barnacles on a boat! I yell, "Peg Leg is his name!" I look around, but everyone seems confused. "Because fish don't have any legs," I explain.

My friends smile and nod, but the boys all shake their heads. "Fin is way better," Cole says.

Ms. Corazón says, "Students, you are very creative, so we have several names to consider. I think we should vote to decide which name is the most popular choice. It's time to go to lunch now, so we'll vote when we get back."

The hot lunch is fish sticks. I'm glad Peg Leg is safe in our classroom!

All during lunch, Cole tries hard to get our class to vote for Fin. He goes to every table. He says different things at each table. "Hey, vote for Fin. You know it's the coolest name. Right?" Or, "Fin is a shark name and sharks are awesome." Or "Peg Leg is a dumb name for a fish, so vote for Fin!"

He doesn't come to the table where Lucy, Paula, Cara, and I are sitting.

"Cole isn't goin' to have time to eat his lunch," Paula says. "He is takin' up his lunchtime talkin' too much."

I open up my pink lunch box. Momma has packed me a PBJ sandwich, with my favorite grape jelly. Plus there's a little bag of goldfish crackers!

I gasp when I see them. "Look!" I say. "I think this is a sign that my name will win!"

"We all have to vote for Peg Leg," Lucy says.

I know the name Peg Leg will get four votes, but I sure hope more kids will vote for it, too. We have twenty-one kids in our class, so if eleven kids vote for the name Peg Leg, we won't have to name our fish Fin.

Since I already know we have four votes, I subtract that from eleven. $11 - 4 = 7$. We need seven more votes!

When we get back to our classroom after recess, Ms. Corazón has put a little piece of paper on each desk. She says, "Remember, we are voting for our favorite fish name. The choices are Swimmy, Sushi, Bait, Fin, Charlie, and Peg Leg."

She writes them all down on the board. Then we vote. I carefully write the name PEG LEG down on my paper. Then I pass it to the front.

Ms. Corazón starts to count the votes. I notice her making several little piles. Oh, no! This means some kids voted for the other fish names, too. It seems like the counting takes forever. Finally, our teacher writes the results on the board.

Swimmy – 2 votes

Charlie – 1 vote

Bait – 2 votes

Sushi – 0 votes

Fin – 7 votes

Peg Leg – 9 votes

"Yay!" I shout. "Peg Leg wins!"

Ms. Corazón says, "I think your book report has our class interested in pirates, Kylie Jean. Our fish will be named Peg Leg."

Cole is not happy. I can tell. He looks like a storm cloud. I feel sorry for Cole, but naming our fish Peg Leg makes me the happiest pirate in the whole wide world!

Chapter Eight
X Marks the Spot

I'm pretty excited that our fish's name is Peg
Leg, but I'm even more excited about my big plan
for the weekend. I'm going to have a treasure
hunt! Pirates love treasure maps because they lead
to buried treasure. The whole crew is coming over
tomorrow and I want to be ready to hunt treasure.

Friday afternoon after school, I make our map.
My first mate Lucy and my dog parrot help out.

I start by drawing a pirate ship right where my
house should be.

Lucy asks, "How do you know where to put it?"

"I guess I don't!" I say. Then I remember something important. "We need a compass rose, like we learned about at school." Once we had a week where we learned a lot about maps. That's a really important part of the map—it's how you know which way is north or south or west or east!

Lucy asks, "Can I draw it on the map?"

"Sure," I say.

I pass the paper over to her and she draws the compass on the corner of the paper across from my ship. Then I draw a dotted line around our garage, past the birdbath, and next to the pine tree. Instead of the bird bath, I draw a little lagoon, and I make the pine tree a palm tree.

I show Ugly Brother. "What do you think so far?" I ask.

He barks excitedly, "Ruff, ruff! Ruff, ruff!"

Lucy gives me a thumbs-up. She's the best first mate ever.

I make the dotted line go out onto Peachtree Lane. At the spot where Miss Clarabelle's house is, I draw some mermaids.

"Ooh, I love it!" Lucy gushes.

"What should we put for Cole's house?" I ask.

Lucy suggests, "How about a shark or a skeleton head?"

"I like the shark idea," I say, "because he wanted to name the fish Fin. Good idea!" Then I give her a high five. We make a great team.

Lucy draws some shark fins right where Cole's house would be.

Our dotted line goes right down the middle of the page to the Black house. Lucy shivers. She pokes her finger down right where the house should be and says, "Put the skull there!"

I do. Finally, we sketch a little island with an X in the middle right beside our hideout. Holding up the map, we take a look at it.

"Blimey! It looks like a real treasure map," I exclaim.

Ugly Brother is so excited, he runs around the room and jumps up on the bed.

Now we need to go bury some treasure to dig up tomorrow. I think we need something special, so I get the gold bracelet Granny gave me when I was an itty bitty baby. It is REAL gold!

"That's your good bracelet," Lucy says. "Won't your momma get mad if we bury it?"

I shrug and tell her, "We're gonna dig it right back up."

"It'll get dirty, though," Lucy says.

"You're right," I say. "I better find something to put it in." I look around my room.

I have a little jewelry box, but if we use that, I'll have to take everything out of it. Then I spy a soft pink bag that Lucy gave me. The top ties with a string. I grab it and put the gold treasure inside.

"Perfect!" I exclaim.

"Okay," Lucy says. "Let's go!"

Ugly Brother is snoring on the bed with his tongue hanging out, so we leave our parrot behind. We pack up the little red wagon with my garden gloves and a small shovel. Then we follow the map we made right down the road, past the mermaids, the sharks, and the skull.

Finally, we're in the backyard of the Black house, right beside our hideout.

Sticking the shovel in the ground, I say, "X marks the spot!"

Digging is harder work than I thought it would be. We should have brought Ugly Brother and a bone. He'll dig like crazy if he thinks there's a doggie bone in the ground! Instead he's taking a nap and we're digging and digging.

I take turns with my first mate. The pile of dirt gets higher and higher. The hole gets deeper and deeper.

After a while, we're tired. I lean on the shovel handle and rest while Lucy goes into our hideout to get some water.

She runs right back out and shouts, "All of our crackers and water are gone. The boys found our hideout!"

I throw down the shovel and run inside. I look everywhere, but Lucy is right. Someone took our food and water!

Everything else looks just the way we left it. The pail and the little bench are still in the middle of the room. Two sets of footprints are on the dirt floor, mine and Lucy's.

This is a real mystery!

Then I remember I left our treasure on the ground. When I run back outside, I see Lucy holding the little pink bag. "Don't worry!" she tells me. "I've been keepin' our treasure safe. Was it the boys?"

"I think so," I say. "We better hurry up and bury this treasure!"

Quickly, we mash the pink bag down in the hole and shovel the dirt right on top. Then I put a little white stone on top of the dirt, to mark our spot. If I forget where I buried my good gold bracelet, I'll be in BIG TROUBLE with Momma!

I take off my little gloves and toss them in the wagon. Then I place Daddy's shovel right on top.

"Let's get out of here," Lucy says. "This place is creepy!"

Chapter Nine
Treasure Hunt

The next morning, my crew arrives bright and early for the big treasure hunt.

We all have our pirate hats on, and the parrot is wearing his feathers. I have a pink sash tied around my waist.

Paula stares at me. "I can't believe you are wearing all of your necklaces and rings!" she says. "Did your momma say it was okay?"

I shrug and tell her, "Pirates like to show off their loot."

We gather around the picnic table in my backyard.

"Okay, mateys," I say. "Here's the treasure map. First Mate Lucy and I made it yesterday, and it's a real good one."

"Wow! It looks like a real pirate map," Cara says.

I shout, "Set sail, me mateys!"

Paula grins. "I think I'm finally starting to understand pirate talk," she says. "You mean we're leaving now, right?"

"That's right!" I say. "I mean, aye!"

"I have a surprise," Cara says. She has her hands behind her back. "Kylie Jean, what's a pirate flag called again?"

"You mean the one with a skull and crossbones?" I say. "That's called a Jolly Roger."

Cara brings out her hands. "I made this for us," she says.

I gasp. Cara is holding a Jolly Roger. And it isn't black like the ones you usually see. No, our Jolly Roger is pink!

"That's fantastic, Cara!" I say. "I love it!"

Cara smiles and sticks it into the back of the wagon. "Okay," she says. "Now we're ready!"

My crew and I head out past the pretend lagoon. There are blue jays in it, but we ignore them. Our dog parrot barks "Ruff! Ruff!" and they fly away.

Miss Clarabelle is out working in her yard. She does not look like a mermaid, but we pretend she's one anyway.

Across the street, Cole is standing in his yard with a mean look on his face. He snarls, showing his teeth just like a shark.

"Girls can't be pirates," he shouts. "You just look silly."

I turn and give the order to keep quiet. If we say anything, he might follow us to our hideout!

Once we've passed him, he yells, "Go ahead and run away, little girlie pirates."

We just keep ignoring him. But when I look at my crew, I can tell they don't like what he's saying.

Up ahead of us, the Black house looks kind of like a skull with its peeling white paint. The dark windows are like eyes, and the porch, missing some boards, looks like a toothless grin. I'm glad we're not treasure hunting at night. It would be super spooky!

"Come on, y'all," I say. "We're almost there."

We head to the backyard. I follow the map and look for the little stone I left to mark our spot. But I can't find it.

"I know it was right here," I say, looking closely at the ground.

"Where is it, then?" Paula asks.

"I'm not sure," I answer. I turn around in a circle to look. "I left a pebble to mark the spot."

The whole crew starts looking for the pebble, but it is gone.

Lucy says, "Maybe an animal moved it."

"Animals wouldn't move a rock for no reason," Cara points out.

Suddenly I realize that if I don't find that bracelet, Momma will be really mad at me. That means I'll be in BIG trouble!

"Dig!" I yell. "We gotta find that treasure or I'll walk the plank!"

Lucy and I dig with a shovel, Ugly Brother digs with his paws, and Cara and Paula use the rusty bucket.

We keep digging holes near the spot Lucy and I buried our treasure yesterday, but nothing turns up.

Suddenly, a giant shadow looms over us. A shiver runs down my spine.

When I turn around, I see an old man. He has long white hair and a beard and is wearing a black patch over one eye.

Standing between us and the stranger, Ugly Brother growls, "Grrrr!"

Bravely, Cara asks, "Who are you?"

The man's voice is low and creaky. He says, "I am Bart Black. Who are you and why are you digging all of these holes in my yard?"

Without thinking, I blurt out, "I think your real name is Black Bart and you're a famous pirate."

Ugly Brother growls again, "Grrrr, grrrr!"

Mr. Black laughs deep from his belly. "I'm no pirate, little gal! If I was, I'd have a lot of gold and a parrot," he says. That makes Ugly Brother whimper.

"Did you steal our things?" I ask.

"I found some crackers in the shed," he says. "Were they yours?" I nod. "I'm sure sorry I took them, but they were so tasty!" he says. "I thought maybe they were mine and I'd just forgot about them."

That's when I notice something. Mr. Black found our buried treasure. He has the pink bag in his hand.

"Are you gonna give our treasure back?" I ask.

"Yes ma'am," he says. "That's why I came out here when I saw you diggin' for it." He hands it over and adds, "I bet your momma wouldn't like to know that you buried that pretty bracelet out here."

"No sir," Paula says. "Her momma would be mad."

"I thought nobody lived here," Cara says. She looks up at the big old house. "Why's your house all fallin' to bits?"

Mr. Black looks sad for a minute. Then he explains that he is old, so he can't keep up with the house and the yard anymore. He doesn't have enough money to spend on hiring people to work for him.

All of his family members live too far away to help, and he is all alone. I don't know what that would be like. After all, most everyone I know lives here in Jacksonville!

"I bet it used to be a real nice house," Lucy says kindly.

Mr. Black smiles. "Yep," he says, "a long time ago, this was a beautiful house! I was proud to live in it."

I think for a second. Then I have a great idea! "I bet we could help you clean up your yard," I say, smiling up at Mr. Black.

"Well, that would be right nice of you," Mr. Black says.

Then I get another great idea. "And then maybe you could help us out with some boy trouble we're havin'," I add. "I know how to help out in yards. Miss Clarabelle lets me help her all time." I point out Miss Clarabelle's house.

"That's a real nice yard," Mr. Black says.

"My brother T.J. can come mow your grass for you," I offer. I'll have to explain to T.J. that Mr. Black doesn't have any money. T.J. usually likes to get paid when he works.

Then another great idea hits me like pirates on a ship deck. T.J.'s youth group at church has been helping old folks fix up their houses!

I decide not to say anything to Mr. Black until I talk to T.J. first. Maybe T.J. and his other friends can help!

Ugly Brother is barking. I look at him and he looks at me. Then I remember my manners!

I say, "Mr. Black, may I introduce my other brother, Ugly Brother. He wants to apologize for lookin' like a parrot right now, but we're pirates and we needed a parrot!"

Ugly Brother barks, "Ruff, ruff."

Mr. Black frowns. "He sure does have an unusual name," he says.

"His real name is Bruno," I explain, "but he doesn't like it, not one little bit. He really wants to be called Ugly Brother."

Mr. Black smiles at me. I bet he knows that Ugly Brother thinks he is a person.

"Now, what's this boy trouble you're havin'?" Mr. Black asks.

We all sit on the ground and explain all about the scurvy dogs — I mean, boys — who don't believe that girls can be pirates.

I add, "If those boys could just see you, sir, they'd think you were a real pirate and then you could tell them girls can be pirates, too. Would you do it? Tonight when we go trick-or-treating?"

"Hmm," he says. "I haven't planned for Halloween this year, so I don't have any treats to pass out."

"That's okay," I tell him.

He agrees to pretend to be Black Bart and tell the boys we are pirates! I would like him to say that I am a pirate queen, but that's probably asking too much.

It's lunch time and we have to get home. We're going to carve pumpkins for tonight after we eat lunch. We wave goodbye to Mr. Black, and then I give the orders to go back to the lagoon.

Chapter Ten

Trick or Treat

That afternoon, the girls and I carve pirate pumpkins!

First, Momma cuts a hole in the tops. Then we scrape out all the seeds with Momma's old kitchen spoons. The spoons have long, long handles. Finally, we use markers to draw on pirate faces. T.J. helps me cut the design out on mine. It kind of looks like Mr. Black.

That reminds me about helping him. "Do you ever cut grass for free?" I ask T.J.

"Not really," he replies. "Except for Momma. Why?"

"You know the old Black house at the end of the street?" I ask.

"Yeah," T.J. says. "That creepy old place."

"Well, Mr. Black needs a lawn boy!" I explain.

T.J. stops carving and looks at me. "Someone lives in that creepy old house?"

While he cuts out Cara's jack-o'-lantern, I tell T.J. all about meeting Mr. Black. Cara's pumpkin looks like the Jolly Roger. It has the skull and crossbones on it. Next, he cuts out Lucy's pumpkin. It looks like a happy face.

T.J. laughs the whole time he is cutting out Paula's pumpkin. When he finally turns it around to show us, I laugh and laugh because her pumpkin looks like Ugly Brother.

Cara blushes. "I didn't have any ideas," she explains, "and he was just sitting there, so I carved his face on my pumpkin."

Then my friends' mommas start to come over to pick up my crew so they can get ready to go trick-or-treating. A cool breeze is blowing. When it gets dark, it will be a little chilly. I don't mind, because part of my costume has a coat.

When my friends are gone, I look at T.J. "You never told me if you'd help out Mr. Black," I remind him.

T.J. shrugs. "I could mow his lawn a couple of times," he says. "And I was thinkin', maybe I could mention him to the youth group and we could help him fix up his house a little bit."

I clap my hands. "That would be fantastic!" I say. "Thank you, T.J.!"

A horn honks outside, and T.J. dashes for the door. He yells, "Have fun, Lil' Bit! Save some candy for me."

"Okay," I say. "I'll try not to eat it all."

Then I hear the front door close and a truck drives away. I climb upstairs to my room to put on my costume. My parrot comes, too.

I put on my black jeans, a white ruffled shirt, and my black boots. I tie my sash around my waist. Now I need help.

I holler, "Momma, please come help me!"

I sit on the bed while she brushes my hair and pulls it into a ponytail. Then she uses her black makeup pencil to draw a fancy mustache right on my face! After I tie a pink bandana on my head, I add my black eye patch, just like Mr. Black. Next is my pirate hat with the glitter skull and crossbones on it. The last thing I put on is my long pink coat and all of my jewels.

"You're the cutest pirate I've ever seen!" Momma says. "All you need is a gold hoop earring." She hands me a clip-on one. YAY! I'm the happiest pirate in the whole wide world.

"I love it," I gush. "Thanks, Momma!"

Downstairs, Daddy is surprised by my costume. He says, "I didn't know pirates wore pink!"

"Yes, sir, pirate queens do all the time," I say.

Just then, the doorbell rings. It's Paula and Cara! Paula is a fairy and Cara is a black cat. As soon as Lucy gets here in her cowgirl costume, we can set sail on our own trick-or-treat adventure. Besides, Mr. Black is expecting us.

We decide to wait out in the front yard. I hope I see Cole, so I can dare him to go to the haunted house at the end of the street and knock on the door.

Once Aunt Susie finally brings Lucy, we start to trick or treat.

"Let's go to Cole's house first," I say.

He answers the door wearing a monster costume. He looks at me and snarls, "A pink pirate. No way!"

I wink at Lucy. Then I turn to Cole and say, "Would you think I was a real pirate if I knocked on the door of the haunted house at the end of the street?"

"The old Black house?" he asks. He shivers and nods. "Okay," he says. "But you'll chicken out before you get to the door."

I laugh. "Let's see who the real pirate is and who the chicken is," I say. "Come on. Whoever knocks on the door is the real pirate."

"All right," Cole agrees.

We walk down the street. The closer we get to the Black house, the more jumpy Cole gets. Under the dim glare of the street light, the house looks really scary.

The house is dark. I start to walk up to the porch, but Cole hangs back. He says, "You aren't going to get close enough to win the dare."

"Are you comin' or not?" I ask.

Cara, Paula, and Lucy wait on the sidewalk. They are trying not to laugh. Lucy has her hand over her mouth. Cole probably thinks she is trying not to scream because she is so afraid.

The steps creak as we walk up to the door. I ask, "Are you ready?"

Cole looks up at the house. Then he says, "Come on, Kylie Jean, let's just forget about it."

"No way," I insist. "I'm gonna prove to you that I'm a pirate queen."

I knock hard on the door three times. Nothing happens at first, and Cole seems relieved.

Then we both hear the faint sound of footsteps coming, and Cole looks like he just swallowed my dog parrot. The door swings open.

Cole takes one look at Mr. Black, whose tall body fills the doorway. When Cole sees the eye patch, he starts to run.

Mr. Black and I watch him run away.

"I'm sorry," Mr. Black says. "I didn't get the chance to tell him that girls can be pirates, too."

"Don't worry," I say, smiling up at him. "Now he knows I'm the bravest pirate."

"And one of the nicest," Mr. Black tells me.

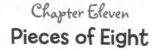

Chapter Eleven
Pieces of Eight

My crew of girl pirates and I go all over the neighborhood gathering candy loot. Granny and Pappy give us extra candy, so we go back and share some with Mr. Black.

Before long we have been to every house with a porch light on and it is getting late. Aunt Susie will be waiting to take Lucy home. We walk past Cara's house and drop her off. Paula's house is on the next street. My first mate Lucy and I are home by eight-thirty.

When Momma sees the candy piled over the top of my bag, she says, "You better share some of that candy with your brothers. Don't give Ugly Brother any chocolate. It's not good for dogs."

"Yes, ma'am," I say.

Momma sends me upstairs to take a bath and change into my PJs. Tonight I get to stay up late, and so Ugly Brother and I sort our loot. There are piles of candy all around me. My dog parrot keeps sniffing around, but he's already had eight pieces of candy. That reminds me that gold coins are called pieces of eight.

When T.J. comes home, I am still awake. I hear him come clomping upstairs. He looks in my room, sees all the candy, and asks, "Where's my share?"

"Come on in so you can pick out your own pieces of eight," I tell him.

Ugly Brother is running around the room, jumping on the bed, and rolling. I think he ate too much sugar. I did, too, or I'd be asleep already.

T.J. winks at me and says, "It looks like you gave Ugly Brother more than eight pieces!"

"Not eight pieces," I explain. "Pieces of eight. Gold coins!"

"More pirate talk, Lil' Bit?" he asks.

I say, "Yup! Just call me Kylie Jean, the Pirate Queen, because now everyone knows girls can be pirates!"

T.J. laughs, takes another piece of candy, and says, "Candy Queen is more like it!"

Marci Bales Peschke was born in Indiana, grew up in Florida, and now lives in Texas with her husband, two children, and a feisty black-and-white cat named Phoebe. She loves reading and watching movies.

When **Tuesday Mourning** was a little girl, she knew she wanted to be an artist when she grew up. Now, she is an illustrator who lives in South Pasadena, California. She especially loves illustrating books for kids and teenagers. When she isn't illustrating, Tuesday loves spending time with her husband, who is an actor, and their two sons.

Glossary

biography (bye-OG-ruh-fee)—a book that tells someone's life story

challenge (CHAL-uhnj)—to invite a person to fight or try to do something

code (KODE)—a set of rules

hideout (HIDE-out)—a place where someone can hide

loot (LOOT)—collection of valuables, sometimes stolen

mysterious (miss-TIHR-ee-uhss)—very hard to explain or understand

oath (OHTH)—a serious, formal promise

occasions (uh-KAY-zhuhnz)—times when something happens

presentations (pree-zen-TAY-shuhnz)—demonstrations of ideas

sailor (SAY-lur)—someone who works on a ship as a member of the crew

sharpshooter (SHARP-shoo-tur)—a person who is very skilled at shooting

Talk!

1. Kylie Jean wanted to prove that girls can be pirates. What else could she have done?

2. Talk about girls and boys. Do you think there are things that girls can do that boys can't, or that boys can do that girls can't? Explain your answer.

3. What do you think happens after this story ends? Talk about it!

Be Creative!

1. Kylie Jean's goal is to be a beauty queen. What's your number-one dream?

2. Who is your favorite character in this story? Draw a picture of that person. Then write a list of five things you know about them.

3. Draw your own pirate map, using your neighborhood as inspiration!

This is the perfect treat for any cupcake queen!
Just make sure to ask a grown-up for help.

Love, Kylie Jean

From Momma's Kitchen

PIRATE'S LOOT COOKIES

YOU NEED:

1 tube of premade cookie dough, sugar cookie flavor

White frosting

Food coloring in jewel tones and yellow

Sugar sprinkles, if desired

A cookie sheet

A grown-up helper

1. Ask your grown-up to bake the cookies as directed, but make them smaller than normal (about the same size as a silver dollar). Cool completely.

2. While the cookies cool, mix small amounts of frosting with food coloring, creating many different colors. Mix each color in its own bowl.

3. Decorate each cookie with one color. Green cookies can be emeralds, red cookies can be rubies, and yellow cookies can be gold coins. Add sprinkles if desired.

Yum, yum!

THE FUN DOESN'T STOP HERE!

Discover more at www.capstonekids.com

♥ Videos & Contests
✿ Games & Puzzles
♥ Friends & Favorites
✿ Authors & Illustrators

Find cool websites and more books like this one at www.facthound.com. Just type in the Book ID: **9781404875814** and you're ready to go!